MW00950814

"Special thanks to my parents who always encouraged my adventures, my writing and my dreams."

DESMOND AND HIS MIGHTY ADVENTURES
By Rebecca Guerrero

www.themightyadventures.com
Cover design and illustrations by Andrew Miller
FIRST EDITION

DESMOND
&
HIS MIGHTY ADVENTURES

Written by
Rebecca Guerrero

Illustrated by
Andrew Miller

Desmond was a little boy as tough as tough could be
and on this very special day Desmond was turning three.

"Little Desmond," his parents said, "we have something for you."

They handed him a birthday gift wrapped in bright, bright blue.

He sat down to open it wondering what it could be.

It was a bear with big brown eyes both soft and cuddly.

"Thank you mom and dad," he said,

"but I'm afraid that you don't see."

"This teddy bear is not tough enough,

not tough enough for me."

"Little Desmond," his parents said, "you're tough,

yes this is true."

"Perhaps your teddy bear can be tougher, just like you."

Desmond headed to his room but his confidence was grim,

when his teddy bear sprang from his arms and ran ahead of him.

His teddy bear ran ahead to the bedroom door.

He gestured for Desmond to follow him. He wanted to explore.

Little Desmond could not believe what he came to see.

He stepped into a jungle where he thought his room should be!

He and Teddy marched around amazed at what they saw,
monkeys swinging from the trees and elephants stood tall.

Desmond was feeling mighty tough, as tough as tough could be

when a lion pounced in front of them with a ROAR that

shook the trees.

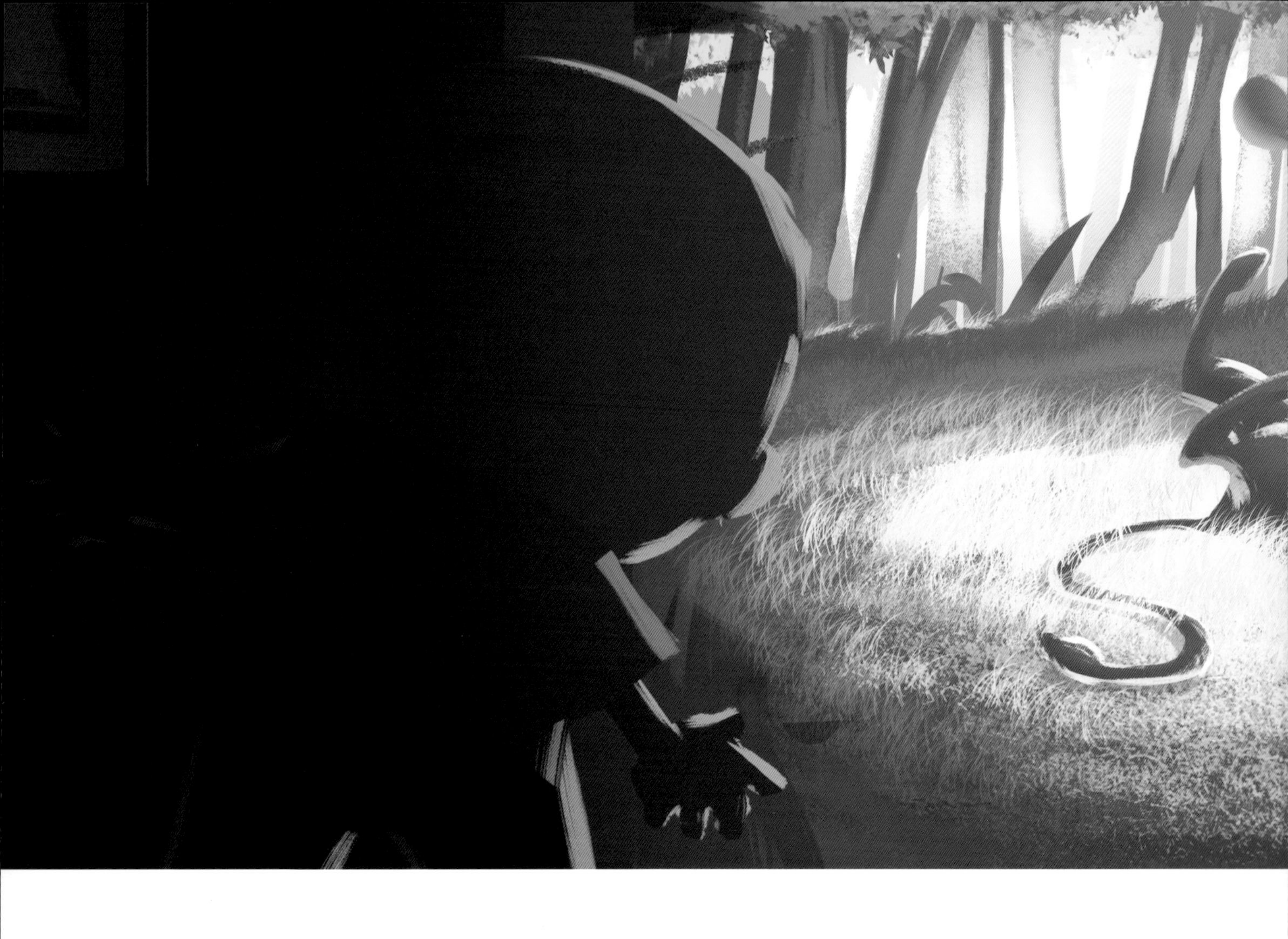

Thinking fast they made a plan and tossed him

Desmond's ball.

That lion was quite ferocious but not scary much at all.

Next Teddy led them down the hall where they heard a BOOM.

There was something waiting there and

they would find out soon.

Desmond called out to his bear, "Can you kindly tell to me,

why is there a pirate ship where the tub should be?"

Teddy stared right back at him, did Desmond see a grin?

Then Teddy climbed aboard the ship and Desmond followed him.

He and Teddy marched around amazed at what they found,

treasure chests and fishing nets and gold stacked by the pound.

Desmond was feeling mighty tough, both tough and out to sea,

but he missed the pirates watching, mad as mad could be.

Desmond fought them with his sword and Teddy threw a net.

The pirates were quite feisty, but these two they'd never get!

Quickly they jumped from the ship and rolled into the hall.

The pirate men were fearsome but not scary much at all.

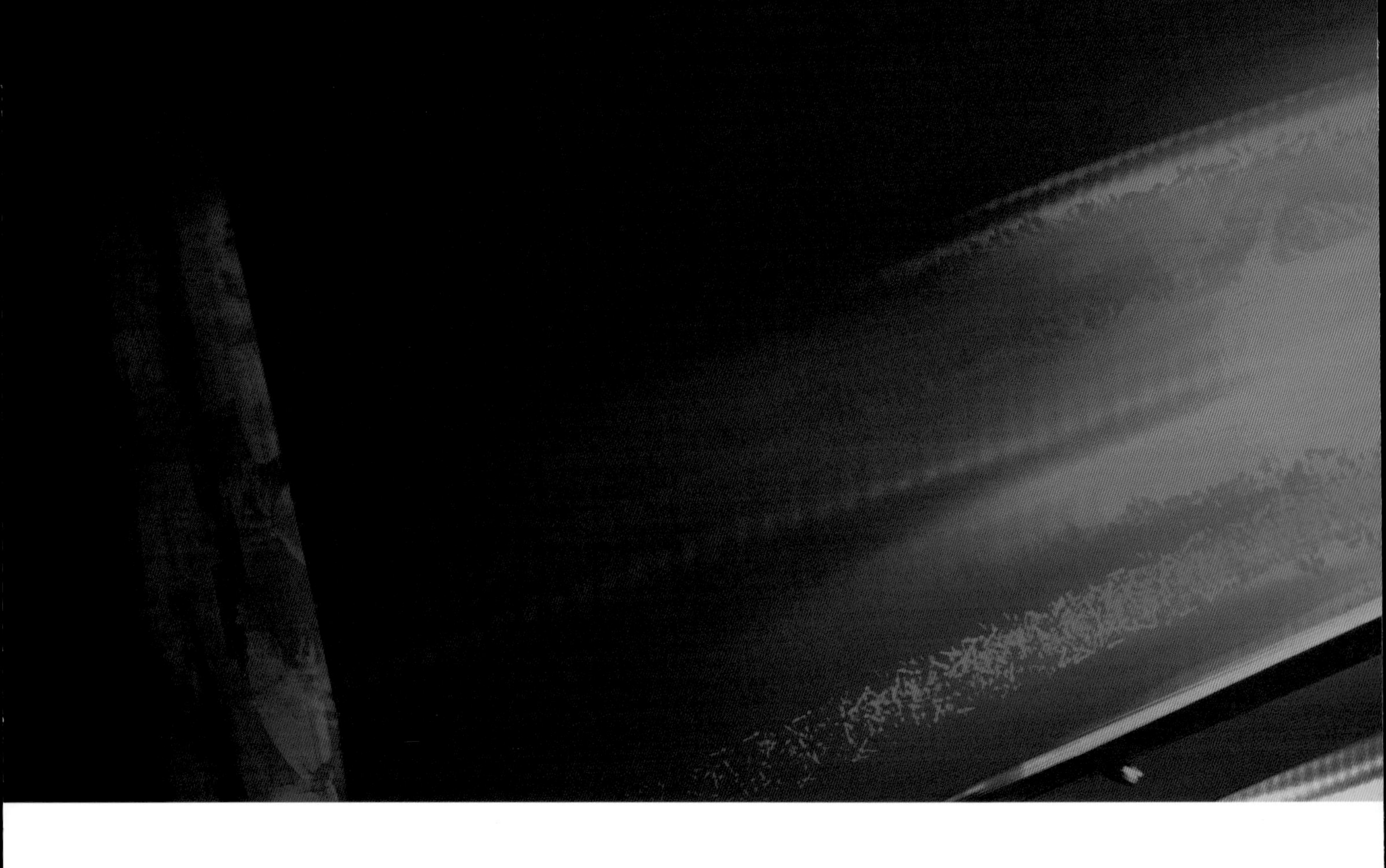

Teddy got up right away and so did Desmond too.

Together they went down the stairs to find something to do.

"I've got this one," Desmond said, as tough as he could be.

"Let's go beyond the basement door and find out what we see."

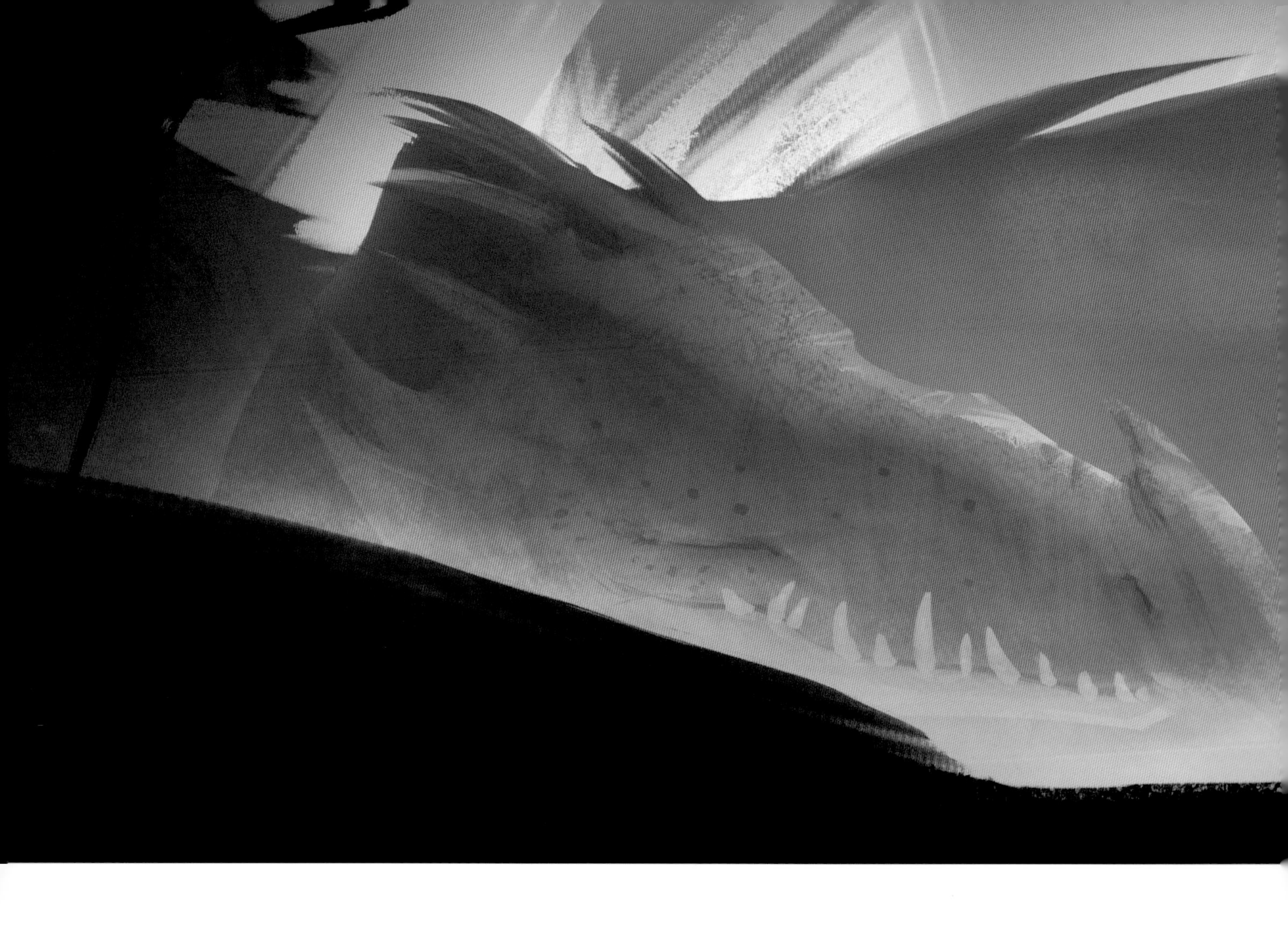

They crept into the darkness ready to explore.

The basement felt very big, far bigger than before.

He and Teddy looked around. What?! It could not be! They found a dragon sleeping right where Desmond's bike should be.

They could hear it breathing loud and could feel the heat.

The fire was inside him as his dragon's heart beat, beat.

Desmond was feeling mighty tough, as tough as tough could be,

but the cave was very dark, too dark for them to see.

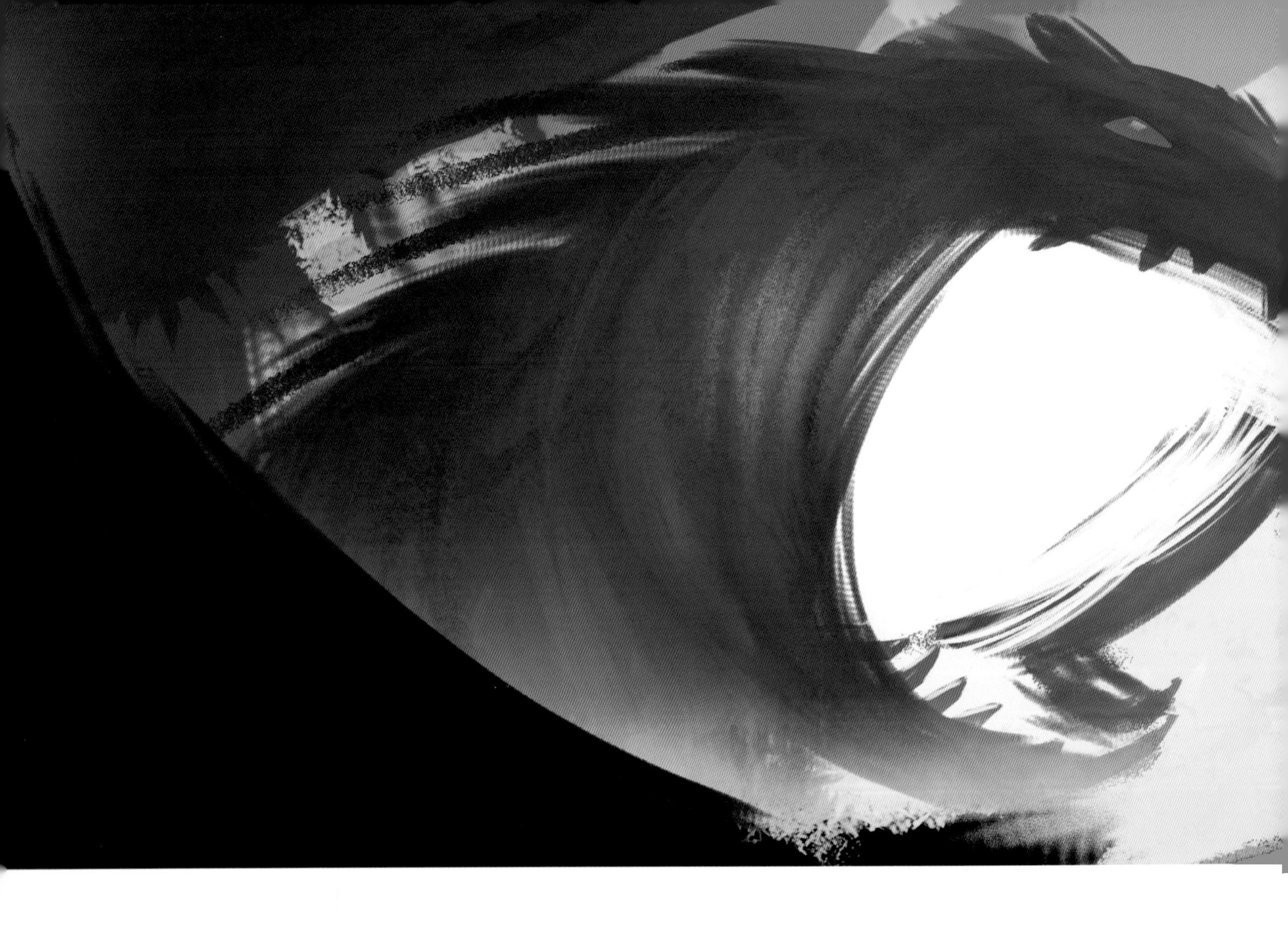

Teddy got snagged in a claw and Desmond soon fell too.
The dragon woke up very fast, there was nothing they could do.

Desmond went straight for his sword but Teddy pulled him back.

Sometimes the braver action is to avoid attack.

The dragon was very fierce and very, very tall,

but it didn't scare them much, not very much at all.

Desmond and Teddy marched upstairs ready for a break.

It was perfect timing, Desmond's parents brought out cake.

"Little Desmond," his parents said, "we know that you are tough.

We'll take back the teddy bear and buy you something rough."

"It's okay mom and dad, on second thought you see,

my teddy bear is very tough. He's tough as tough can be!"

"We're very glad you like him," they sat down by their son.

"Happy birthday Desmond, you and Teddy go have fun."

Desmond was feeling mighty tough, as tough as tough could be
but it was far more fun being tough with his teddy.

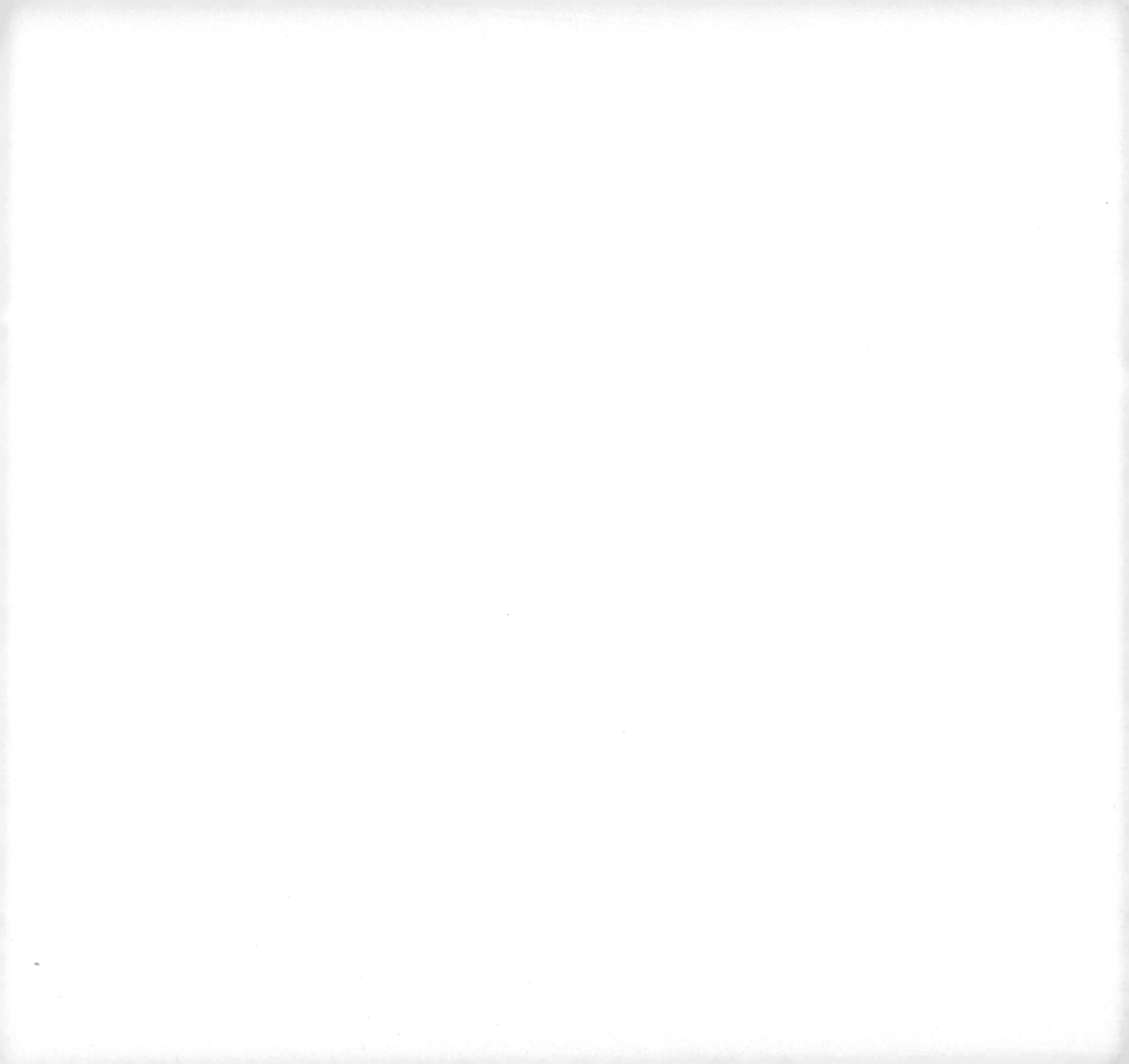